Animal Stories

Featuring The Missing Pony, Wilfred Wolfred & The Butterfly Garden

igloo

The Missing Pony

Gemma was stuck on the second level of her computer game. "You're not still playing that, are you?" said her mother, coming into her bedroom. "It's such a lovely day out. Why don't you get some fresh air instead?"

Gemma groaned. She hated going out lately because that meant walking past the empty field by the side of the house. The field hadn't always been empty. Two months ago it had been home to Merry, a beautiful little roan pony, but a horse thief had come along one winter's night, and now the pony was gone.

Tears stung Gemma's eyes, but she refused to cry any more. She went down the stairs and gave a soft whistle. In a flash of brown and white, her little terrier, Benji, came charging at her, wagging his tail furiously. A walk might cheer her up. Gemma and Benji headed to the place they always went: a smooth flat rock at the top of the hill that overlooked the town. Gemma let her thoughts drift to Merry. She missed her little pony so much. She missed riding her and nuzzling her neck.

Gemma was lost in her thoughts when the sound of Benji yapping made her snap out of it. In the distance, Gemma could make out a figure coming from the woods.

As the figure got closer she saw the girl scoop the little dog into her arms.

She was worried until she recognized who it was – Mary Donnolly, a girl she knew a little from school.

Although Gemma and Mary were in the same class, the girls didn't know each other very well at all. Gemma's friends all thought that Mary was a bit strange and avoided her. It was true that Mary was a little different from the other girls. She wore slightly odd clothes, and she was always on her own, reading books about plants and animals.

Some of the other girls joked that Mary could do magic, but Gemma thought that was mean, so she always gave her a smile when they passed in the corridor.

As she walked up the hill with the runaway terrier tucked under her arm, Mary recognized Gemma as one of the popular girls at school. But unlike the other girls, who nudged each other and whispered as Mary walked past, Gemma had always seemed kind.

As the classmates drew closer they smiled shyly, but when Mary handed over the little dog she wondered why she saw such sadness in Gemma's eyes. "What's wrong?" she asked. "You look like you're missing something."

Gemma was startled by Mary's keen observation. "I'm thinking about my missing pony," she replied without thinking. Mary gave an understanding nod, but Gemma blushed. Why had she shared her secret with someone she hardly knew? "Bye for now," she smiled awkwardly, turning to leave. "See you at school."

As Mary headed down the hill she was lost in thought. She could not forget the sadness in Gemma's eyes. "I must do my best to help her," she whispered.

When she got home, Mary went straight to her herb garden and picked a sprig of sweet-smelling rosemary.

"For remembrance," she smiled, as she put it in her basket. Next she picked lucky lavender, and a handful of dandelions puffballs. Mary smiled to herself. She had a special gift. She used natural remedies to cure sick animals. And there was something else, too, which she couldn't quite explain. When she made wishes, they sometimes came true. She knew the others at school found her odd and shy, and this made her unpopular. But she didn't know how to change things. And no amount of wishing for friends of her own seemed to help. Her wishes only seemed to work for others . . .

That evening, Mary wove the rosemary and lavender into a ring around a pot, and put the dandelions in the middle. Then she sat down to think about Gemma and her lost pony. Mary held up the pot in the moonlight and gently blew. The dandelion seeds drifted away on the cool night breeze as Mary made a wish.

In a nearby valley a little roan pony was falling asleep in her stall when the cool night breeze stirred her. She sniffed and began to wake up. Her new owners worked her so hard that she was always so tired these days, but suddenly she felt she could shake off her exhaustion. She was restless. She started to paw the floor, then she started to kick the door. Finally she used her hind legs to smash the door off its hinges, and ran out into the night.

Gemma never knew how her beloved Merry came to be whinnying under her bedroom window that night. She never found out where she had been or who had taken her. But she didn't really care. She only cared that she was home and her heartache was over.

But there was one thing about the day her pony came home that nagged at her. When she had locked eyes with strange little Mary Donnelly on the hillside, she had seen compassion and wisdom, but also something else; loneliness.

Gemma nuzzled Merry's soft, velvety nose and hugged her silky, smooth neck, then leaped up onto her newly saddled back. As they headed off towards the woods, Gemma urged Merry into a trot and called for Benji to catch up. "Come on boy," she called to the little dog. "We're off to make a new friend."

Wilfred Wolfred

Wilfred Wolfred was a Big Bad Wolf who was trying to be good. But today he was having a bad day.

First he stubbed his toe on the table leg. Then he went to make toast and found the bread was stale. And then it got worse and worse. By mid-morning he had lost his handkerchief when he went out for a walk. By lunchtime he had torn a hole in his best shirt!

Wilfred wondered what he had done to deserve such bad luck, especially since he had been good all week long . . .

On Monday, he heard that Mrs. Red Riding Hood was having trouble with her plumbing. So, now that he was a good wolf, he gathered his tools and went to help her.
"I'm so glad to see you!" cried Mrs. Red Riding Hood. "There's a hole under my sink and the water is flooding my kitchen."

Wilfred Wolfred took his tools and after much huffing and muttering he managed to mend the hole in the pipe.

On Tuesday, he'd promised to help Mrs. Little Pig repair her roof. He tried not to puff too much as he mended the thatch on the roof, for fear of it blowing down again.

On Wednesday, he got a phone call from Mrs. Goat. Her grandfather clock was going wrong and kept chiming all the time and waking her kids up. Now Wilfred was feeling rather tired, but since he was now a good wolf he forced himself out of bed and went to help. Luckily it was only a white mouse that was stuck inside it, so he didn't have to stay

too long. This was a great relief for the seven little goats, as they were sure that Wilfred Wolfred was going to gobble them up.

On Thursday, Wilfred went for a walk. As he passed underneath a very tall tree he heard cries. Stuck at the top of the tree was The Boy Who Cried Wolf. Even though he was very hungry and wasn't at all sure the boy was really stuck, Wilfred climbed up to help. And though his mouth watered, and he could have easily gobbled up the boy without anyone noticing, he didn't.

Now, here he was on Friday having a Big Bad Day. He'd done nothing but good deeds all week, and yet he was having the worst luck. He felt very annoyed. What was the point of being good if bad things happened to him?

Wilfred Wolfred

"Maybe if I go back to being bad, good things will happen to me?" he thought to himself.
And that's exactly what he set out to do!

First of all he decided to pay Mrs. Red Riding Hood a visit.

When he peeked through the window he saw that she was busy taking something out of the stove, so he crept around the other side, where he saw Little Red Riding Hood. She was all by herself in the garden.

So he crept behind the bush, and was just about to pounce, when . . .
"Ah, Wilfred Wolfred!" came a voice. Wilfred stood up quickly, looking
sheepish. Well, wolfish.
It was Mrs. Red Riding Hood.
"I was just coming to find you. I've made you a chocolate cake to thank
you for helping me mend my leaky sink," she said.

So Wilfred wolfed down a huge piece of the cake and thanked
Mrs. Red Riding Hood.

Wilfred still felt he should do something big and bad. So he decided to
pay a visit to the Little Pigs' house.

Mrs. Little Pig was inside the house sewing. While she wasn't looking
he crept into the garden where the three little pigs were sleeping in the
sunshine. His mouth watering, he was just about to pounce, when . . .

"Ah, Wilfred Wolfred, the very wolf I wanted to see!" came a voice.

Wilfred stood up quickly, looking very red-faced.
"Oh, good afternoon Mrs. Little Pig" he replied.
"I was just coming to find you, to see if you needed any sewing done
and to thank you for helping me fix my roof," she said.

So Wilfred went to get his best shirt with the hole in it, and thought
how lucky it was that he hadn't gobbled up her sons, or his shirt would
never have been mended.

After that he decided to pay a visit to Mrs. Goat.
He was just on his was way when . . .

"Wilfred Wolfred!" shouted a voice. It was the Boy Who Cried Wolf,
running towards him.

"Oh, here comes a tasty snack," thought Wilfred. "Maybe I will get to be bad after all."

He was just about to pounce, when he saw something. The Boy Who Cried Wolf was holding his handkerchief.

"I saw it from the top of the tree," he panted. "I wanted to return it as a thank you for saving me."

Wilfred Wolfred thanked the boy. He liked the handkerchief.

He was just about to set out again to Mrs. Goat's house to be really big and bad, when he thought about all the nice things that had happened that day. His tummy was full of chocolate cake. His best shirt had been mended, and his handkerchief had been returned. And his toe hardly hurt at all any more. His big bad day was actually turning out rather well. And it wasn't because he had done anything big and bad, it was because of the good things he had done.

So, then and there, he decided to turn back into a Big Good Wolf. And he would never think about gobbling anyone up ever again.

Well, hardly ever.

The Butterfly Garden

Lottie, Sam and Michelle were the best of friends. One day, just before school ended for the summer, they were wandering home along the lane that led to their road, when all at once they stopped. Dancing in front of them was the most beautiful butterfly they had ever seen.

"It's so pretty!" whispered Sam. "I wish I was a butterfly."

Another butterfly appeared, then another, and another. There were butterflies everywhere. "Let's follow them!" cried Lottie, grabbing her friends' hands.

The girls followed the fluttering trail through the park and into the town, until they came to a door in a wall behind the bus stop. The door was slightly ajar.

"Do you think we should follow them?" whispered Michelle.

"Absolutely!" cried Lottie.

The girls stepped into a sun-drenched public garden.

"Oh!" gasped Sam. "It's beautiful!"

The velvety lawn was divided by archways dripping with flowers. Right in the middle was a pond with a fountain. Everywhere the girls looked, there were butterflies and other creatures. Birds sang and dragonflies hummed as the girls wandered along the walkways, breathing in the scent of a thousand flowers.

"I don't think I've ever been anywhere as beautiful as this said Lottie. I can't believe it was just sitting here in the middle of town all this time."

The girls sat in the garden and looked around for a long time, until their tummies began to rumble and they remembered it was nearly time for supper. Only then did they reluctantly go home.

Lottie, Sam and Michelle visited the garden almost every day that summer. They had picnics, played games, and chatted while watching the butterflies dance around. It was their secret.

One Sunday, towards the end of the summer, Sam was having lunch with her family. Sam's dad was talking about a new shopping mall that was going to be built in the middle of town.

The Butterfly Garden

They were going to build it right on top of the garden. The news upset Sam so much, she could barely finish her lunch. Their beautiful secret garden was going to be destroyed. It was more than she could bear.

Later that day, Sam met her friends at the garden as usual, and told them the terrible news.
"We've got to do something!" cried Lottie. "This must be why the butterflies led us here, so that we could save their garden!"
"But what can we do?" asked Michelle. "Who will listen to us?"

Lottie was adamant. "We have to try. We can't let it be destroyed."
All afternoon, the girls discussed ways to save the garden.

"I know," said Lottie.

"Why don't we organize a party at the garden?"
"Great idea!" the others agreed. "Then everyone can see how special it is."

The girls spent the rest of the week making invitations, which they mailed to everyone they could think of: friends, parents, teachers – even the mayor.

When the day of the party arrived, the girls spent the whole morning preparing food and drinks for their guests. They borrowed chairs and tables and arranged them around the garden.

Finally they hung banners from the trees that said "Save the Butterfly Garden!"

As the guests arrived, the three friends showed them around, and told them about the shopping mall.

Everybody who saw the garden agreed that it had to be saved, and they all signed a petition. Soon the girls had over one hundred signatures. At the end of the afternoon, the girls approached the mayor, who was sitting admiring the fountain.

"Excuse me," said Lottie nervously. "We'd like to present you with our petition to save this garden."

"Thank you," said the mayor kindly, "but I'm afraid that the plans have already been approved.

I'm sorry, but the decision is out of my hands at this stage. So, girls, unless you can come up with a miracle, this wonderful garden will be knocked down." And with a sad smile the mayor left.

The three girls started to clear up all the leftovers.
"It's not fair," sighed Michelle, gazing at a blue butterfly, sitting on the rim of a cup she was holding. "Why are buildings more important than a beautiful butterfly like this?"
Lottie turned to look. A strange expression came over her face.
"Don't move, Michelle," she whispered. "Sam! Quick!
Bring me my camera. I think that butterfly is a Cornhill Beauty. It's a very rare species. I saw one in my wildlife book the other day."